# MESMERIZING MANIZALEN MAMACITAS

BY
AIYSHA SWALLOWGREN

ISBN: 979-8-9878596-6-7
First Printing July 2025
Printed in United States of America

# Contents

Able / 5, Anything / 6, Bad Butterfly / 7, Bark / 8, Beach / 9, Beer / 10,
Blessed / 11, Bolder / 12, Broomstick / 13, Bus Ride / 14, Bust / 15,
Butterfly Tear / 16, Caring / 17, Catastrophe / 18, Clutch / 19,
Complete / 20, Construction / 21, Crotch Shot / 22, Dancing / 23,
Defile / 24, Dignified / 25, Dignity / 26, Disciplining / 27,
Discretion / 28, Disgust / 29, Drained / 30, Drool / 31, Dumping / 32,
Dusted / 33, Eater / 34, Encore / 35, Engineer / 36, Expert / 37,
Feline / 38, Ferris Wheel / 39, Flooding / 40, Flowed / 41, Freedom / 42,
Freezing / 43, Gap / 44, Gentle / 45, Gently / 46, Gravy Train / 47,
Gushing / 48, Hit / 49, Hot and Heavy / 50, Ice Cream / 51,
Inner Space / 52, Jill / 53, Leniency / 54, Lesson / 55, Levitate / 56,
Mess / 57, Milkshake / 58, Misconduct / 59, Missed / 60, Mist / 61,
Molten / 62, Mother's Day / 63, Moving / 64, Neon / 65, Nights / 66,
Organic / 67, Path / 68, Pitbull / 69, Plain / 70, Plaything / 71,
Pressure / 72, Pride / 73, Provoker / 74, Public / 75, Punching Bag / 76,
Relaxing / 77, Roughed / 78, Rule / 79, Salivate / 80, Sandwich / 81,
Sea / 82, Side / 83, Silent / 84, Sky Moon / 85, Slant / 86, Sleeping / 87,
Slingshot / 88, Squirt / 89, Strategy / 90, Striking / 91, Sucker / 92,
Sunflower / 93, Syrup / 94, Telling / 95, Thunder / 96, Tired / 97,
Track / 98, Turn / 99, Twisted / 100, Ufff / 101, Weekend / 102,
Wet / 103, Working / 104, Yearn / 105

# ABLE

She didn't know how his imagination was able
To make her resolve and her lap unable
To stop leaking, his hands under the table
Doing things that make her blush, so shameful
He was the one that taught her pleasure from painful
Treatment and he opened her mind until she was able
To be a total slut, in Sharpie he would label
Her and then start collecting her juices in a ladle
At the restaurant he ordered a plain bagel
Then covered it in her juices as she starts to cradle
His balls but her breathing is getting unstable
She didn't think she could be this nasty, but he showed her she was able

# ANYTHING

For her master's pleasure she would do anything
Provoking him by encouraging him to bring
Many of his friends and use her as their plaything
She blindfolded herself and laid back in the sex swing
Enjoying how his belt made it sting
Oh so hotly she was ready for anything
As her breath shortened as he started to wring
Her naughty neck as her tongue would spring
Out for more cum, she loves serving her king
He fucked her so hard it broke her bedspring
She always remembers the dirtiest thing
He did to her; it was hotter than anything

# Bad Butterfly

She said please keep my secret, I'm a bad butterfly
My giant hands lifting her into the sky
My leather belt hitting her harshly on the thigh
The worse he behaved, the more her desires multiply
He was letting her be a free, wild, bad butterfly
She user lots of saliva when she found me dry
Taking some rope and starting to tie
Her up with the video recording so many can spy
She begged for rudeness, so I spit in her eye
Any desire I have she is eager to comply
Anything for her big boy, there's nothing she will deny
Me especially deepthroating as she starts to cry
Sir you are turning me into an even nastier bad butterfly

# Bark

She had never thought about starting to bark
He leashed her in the back of the park
The thoughts bubbling over with dark
Desires his spankings igniting a spark
He tossed her around like a little Monarch
Then he ordered her to loudly bark
She learned that she had a new favorite remark
From him he said bark bitch and made her back arc
She swallowed his seal like a tiger shark
Now he has tied her up at home plate in the ballpark
The team celebrating as they start to embark
On running a train on this bitch, bitch I said bark

# BEACH

She's very excited to go to the beach
She will savor every second each
And every second as she knows he can teach
Her new angles to play with her peach
The warm sun heating her body on the beach
Listening to the ocean, such natural speech
She yearns for him to collar and leash
Her and together they smoke hashish
She is so excited to finally reach
The ocean it turns her on tanning on the beach

# Beer

She first had a margarita then started to have a beer
She posed with it seductively, whispering dear
I want you to drink me like this, is that clear
Enough then she guided me to touch here
Interesting things pop up and it would appear
That obviously we are going to need another beer
She worked very hard and had an interesting career
She said please hurt me in the most severe
Ways and the longing in her voice was sincere
She uses her mouth to make things disappear
The thing she does that fills me with the most cheer
Is when she bends over and shows off her hot rear
She shakes it hotly while drinking another beer

# Blessed

In dark times she always makes me feel blessed
Another love note, he cordially addressed
Her and whispered I never can stay depressed
When I think about my mood is the best
Someone that truly listens always impressed
Her and when it comes to her pleasure I'm obsessed
She is very obliging, happy to fulfill any request
Sometimes she is shocked at what I suggest
I dressed as a priest as she hotly confessed
To what she had done to her teacher to pass her test
She said how excited she becomes when she expressed
That her darkest longings could no longer be repressed
She put on a collar handed me the leash and begged to be possessed
There's so much saliva, my pet is truly blessed

# BOLDER

She loved when he started acting bolder
The way he spoke to her made her smolder
She giggled as he tossed her over his shoulder
His hands knew which buttons to press on her controller
Making her feel very young even though she was older
She got very warm when he showed her
An entirely new definition of bolder
Whispering that beauty is in the eye of the beholder
Her eyes growing as he demanded her to call him sir
Rubbing her thighs, making her purr
When he grabs her hair, the wildest thoughts occur
He had ways of creating thoughts most impure
And it made her beg for him to be even bolder

# Broomstick

He fell in love with a bruja, she rode his broomstick
To magical places like when his candle wick
Started lighting a new type of magic trick
He talked deeply making her as slick
As an oil spill and she was quick
To start moving her hips against her broomstick
He poured more molten lava using his dipstick
Wound up her clock just to watch her tick
Ordered her sit on his face and started to lick
Her covering her lap like ants at a picnic
Then she started doing things that ruined her lipstick
Another magical adventure on her firm broomstick

# Bus Ride

She and her master went on a bus ride
When the lights dimmed his hand started to glide
Soon it was a messy game of slip and slide
She shuddered as his hand started to go inside
Her lap as the feelings and wetness multiplied
He slid into her ass slowly during the bus ride
Hand over her mouth as her eyes grew wide
A few Men noticed and she did nothing to hide
That she was a devoted pet and always complied
It just turned her on that they spied
Tears ruining her makeup as he applied
More pressure this was a hot joyride
When the bus stopped her took her outside
Now she's covered in cum, it has dried
She wore his treat on her face for the rest of the bus ride

# Bust

He is worshipping her beautiful bust
He saw her excitement and as she cussed
He added much more depravity to her lust
Taking the back of her head and starting to thrust
Deeper and deeper as she begs him to bust
Another load in her stomach he didn't rush
As she swallowed it made her insides combust
The thoughts that used to fill her with disgust
Now make her excited nipples puffed
She found out she was longing to be handcuffed
With him she found someone she could trust
She could always trust him to make her bust

# BUTTERFLY TEAR

I get really worked up licking a butterfly tear
She let me relax by slowly starting to smear
Her lipstick on my lap this is my dear
Little pet butterfly, she's got a great rear
Which I spank repeatedly, another butterfly tear
Shed as his hands slowly veer
Around her neck, I make it quite clear
That she gets too turned on from fear
I keep taking her to a new frontier
Making her embrace her favorite career
She sucked, slobbered, and serviced my spear
Mascara running down her face as I make it disappear
Licking her new gift for me, a fresh butterfly tear

# CARING

She was extraordinarily good at caring
For him and he found himself staring
At such warm eyes she's pairing
Them with cool sunglasses no comparing
Her with anyone else she is my definition of caring
I show her my rainbow heart baring
My soul with moonlight vibes airing
Out the negative using her to keep repairing
Trust and she makes it safe to start sharing
Space I like that you make me more daring
Is there a big smile on your face are you wearing
That warmth mamacita you're very caring

# CATASTROPHE

He knew just how to give her a catastrophe
Get her riled up and do it so tactfully
He knew that there was something about how casually
He would give her glimpses of his rascally
Ways and he loved giving her a surprising catastrophe
He pushed her favorite buttons happily
She did start breathing ever so rapidly
He licked new places and found a new galaxy
Making her blush as she has another tragedy
She found in herself a new level of depravity
At the same time, he raised her spirituality
With a simple whisper he can make a real catastrophe

# CLUTCH

He came through for her clutch
She was not used to being this way such
A wild imagination he had and a refined touch
He started hitting her ass with her hairbrush
There was something about how easily he can clutch
Her like a little doll and covering her mouth, shush
His hand around her neck making her quite flush
Leaking and creaming a most delicious mush
He painted her face with his thick paintbrush
Recording her being a bitch, ruining her blush
She would do anything for a man that came in clutch

# COMPLETE

He listens very carefully, giving his complete
Attention as he made sure to greet
Her with warmth, she found him very sweet
She surprised him by treating him like a piece of meat
She bent over and encouraged his hand to meet
Her ass now she's getting her complete
Desires met and went crazy when he beat
Her as she gagged for his special treat
He lifted her by the neck off her feet
The force he used makes her excrete
Desires as he made her feel very petite
How rough he was with her, his little freak
Made her walk with cum on her face down the street
Now her transformation into a total whore is complete

# CONSTRUCTION

She was dressed in bright orange like construction
Walking into the street causing much disruption
Watching her tone body with no interruption
I start whispering in her ear about rich destruction
I'm a wrecking ball in her mind, new construction
Will start soon if she can just slow the seduction
Down a little there's so much saliva and suction
She learns quickly and so eager for instruction
I'm spanking her ass, pulling her hair, and an eruption
Spewing everywhere, grab a sign that says under construction

# CROTCH SHOT

She is showing me a very naughty crotch shot
She loves showing off, a whole lot
It makes her even hornier when she smokes pot
Being a little whore makes her extremely hot
Bending over she gave her teacher a crotch shot
Saying oops, no panties, I guess I forgot
Opening her backpack, showing me she had brought
A collar for herself as she whispered, I'm not
Going to say no to anything, I desire to be taught
She desperately tries to behave, but cannot
Stop thinking of his hands dipping in her honeypot
Sticky and dripping from another crotch shot
She thinks of her Once Caldas jersey he bought
It makes her stop caring about getting caught
She said I'm yours, anything I've got
So, I slid into her warm and tight slot
Leaking with cum, she takes another crotch shot

# Dancing

The way he treats her makes her feel like dancing
He walks through the door, and she starts prancing
Into his arms as he begins to fling
Her through the air and into her sex swing
Now she's ready for some exotic dancing
Moving her hips and loudly panting
She gets so excited being his plaything
How easily he turns on her everything
How hot he makes her ready for anything
On her knees eagerly glancing
At him taking his time advancing
Her desires in her lap his tongue starts dancing

# DEFILE

She woke him up by loudly starting to defile
Herself he looked at the growing saliva pile
That woke him up as it has been a while
Since she showed him her filthy style
Dressed as a secretary as she starts to file
He sees she has no panties, ready to defile
Herself for her boss, her body very fertile
He had encouraged her naughty lifestyle
Confessing in church, her dripping down the aisle
Hitting herself hard made her smile
Very much now she's licking the tile
Covered in her juices, she loves to defile

# DIGNIFIED

He showed her treatment that was exceptionally dignified
When it came to pleasure, she let him guide
Her to cravings she had kept hidden deep inside
She relaxed as his large hands started to glide
Down her back as he caressed one side
Of her face and she whispered enough dignified
Treatment sir, so he carefully tied
Her hands and blindfolded her as she tried
To guess how we would make her desires multiplied
So vulnerable with her legs open wide
The pressure around her neck that he applied
Made her very close to cumming but he denied
Her and she reacted in ways most undignified
She begged him to take her outside
She promised to do anything as long as he would provide
The source of depravity nobody would call dignified

# Dignity

She loves when I strip her of her dignity
By punishing her firmly and sufficiently
She found freedom in being treated filthily
I showed her that when smacked skillfully
She was more than happy to surrender her dignity
Treating her as my pet hitting, in captivity
Made her start begging quite ambitiously
She gets hornier the more miserably
She is treated especially when I explicitly
Tell her all the ways I will use my creativity
To destroy every ounce left of her dignity

# DISCIPLINING

She confessed her urges for his disciplining
So he tossed her to the ground in the beginning
As he dragged her by the hair she started grinning
The first slap made her mind start spinning
The paddle said slut and he's imprinting
His little naughty toy, she needs much disciplining
The sheets are so damp she's basically swimming
In a pool of her hot and juicy sinning
He made her experience a new way of living
She learned to receive more by his giving
Her the best and worst of himself he's hitting
Her ass harder and the difficulty is filling
Her darkest desires for tremendous disciplining

# Discretion

She grew to really appreciate his discretion
She said I'll be your student, teach me a lesson
In her mind he answered a very important question
Unleashing her inner freak with a rough session
She encouraged him to use beastly aggression
He had to muzzle her to keep up the discretion
She wore a nun outfit today, eager to give her confession
Becoming sexually deviant was her new obsession
She begged him to consider doing this as a profession
The powerful way he made her come in succession
Using his belt, a smack for each transgression
His beatings were the cure to her depression
She wore a collar with his name, she's his possession
Totally safe, very perverse, with total discretion

# DISGUST

Her neighbors look at her in disgust
With how open her blouse was exposing her bust
No panties obvious as a wind gust
Lifts her skirt and the neighbors must
Know that she is eager to combust
Begging please do difficult things that would disgust
Most women, she enjoys her master's trust
It makes her leak every time they discussed
Naughty and filthy things made her nipples puffed
Now she finds herself covered in spit and handcuffed
She keeps begging to get totally stuffed
Please treat me like a bitch, she cussed
It makes her pussy erupt being such a disgust

# DRAINED

She was eager to leave him totally drained
She begged to be beat, begged to be caned
The harsher he was, the greater she was pained
Made her desire be his bitch, to be chained
And how eager she was to be trained
Anything for master, she was well trained
To let out the whore inside her that was contained
She starts leaking when she is restrained
The filthier she was, the more entertained
He was and every disgusting thing she sustained
Made her a wild animal, she's unrestrained
In her efforts, she loudly proclaimed
For him to do his worst, she was unashamed
To be his little fuckdoll, she'd do anything to leave him drained

# DROOL

She was shocked by how much drool
Accumulated from her mouth, there's a pool
Of it and she bent over to let him jewel
Her ass and she pleaded, sir please be cruel
Make me never dare to break a rule
Use me as your doll,  my holes are a tool
For your relaxation as she watched the drool
Start forming a filthy, gross cesspool
Today she had dressed like she was going to school
She craved disciplining of every molecule
Of her body his tongue causing a whirlpool
She's slipping and sliding, covered in drool

## DUMPING

She moves her hips begging him to start dumping
Another load of warm milk inside her confronting
The realization that there's nothing
More exciting than when his balls start bumping
Against her ass she starts bucking
Riding her cowboy, enthusiastically jumping
His little pet so excited as he starts dumping
Deep inside her then starts smothering
Her and all the spit makes her hair start clumping
His large, firm hands start thumping
Against her body and with her mouth she starts pumping
She is his little cumdump, he keeps dumping

# DUSTED

Dressed as a French maid she carefully dusted
She bent over as he slowly thrusted
Inside her pulling her panties aside she adjusted
To receiving joy from that which previously disgusted
Her and each time that she dusted
She would walk around with his busted
Gift  dripping down her leg until it was encrusted
She gasped as he pulled deeply and combusted
She dreamt of a man that could be trusted
To use her totally while she dusted

# Eater

I love girls that are an eater
Shoving things in their mouths so eager
To fill her plate until the food starts to teeter
When she seems men that are 188cm
She wants to be stamped more than a postage meter
She is a lioness she looks at me like an eater
Of meat she begs to feel like she's meeting the reaper
Sir blow me up like a drug dealer's beeper
I was making an omelet when she stuck the eggbeater
In her ass now there's dessert for the reader
She thoroughly enjoys a man that's a huge eater

# Encore

She wanted a second book, a hot encore
She said let's be more disgusting,  more hardcore
I make her lap hot and her thoughts soar
She would hit very hard,  she will be very sore
She was his little pet, his filthy whore
Spank your ass pet, hit it even more
I'm going to elevate difficulty, a hard encore
She drips as I am licking her backdoor
I know how to make her cum harder than ever before
Send her to watch football, Once Caldas score
A goal makes her so happy and glad to explore
She tries harder than ever, spit covering her floor
Five fingers pushing until she can't take it anymore
The belt around her neck leaving a mark of his encore

# ENGINEER

She was going to school to be an engineer
She walked into class and thought I belong here
Something happened as her teacher came near
Oh this was going to be a most delicious year
Building bridges would be her career
In class her teacher was a sexy engineer
She dropped a note that said sir please smear
My lipstick and sternly punish my rear
He ordered her to detention, it would appear
That she became excited from fear
The first slap so hard it made a tear
Then he used her mouth to make his dick disappear
He was in charge; he made that very clear
Building bridges and exploring a new frontier
She begged to have detention all year
The difficulty was intense the pain severe
Her teacher became her perversion engineer

# EXPERT

She looks forward to hearing from her expert
He would make her mind blurt
Out the most ridiculous fantasies as he would flirt
With her until her excitement pokes through her t-shirt
He was the reason for the dampness under her skirt
She loves it hot and sexy, he's a real expert
At grabbing her hair. using his hands to assert
Who was in control, who makes her a pervert
She's reading this and slowly starting to insert
Something delicious in her mouth, a creamy dessert
She opened wide as he started to spurt
It made him crazy how desperately she begs to be hurt
Showing him that her mouth is also an expert

# Feline

I sat there observing a feral feline
Inside I desired to have her be mine
So, I opened my heart and let it shine
Poured her a large glass of wine
It's liquid catnip for a fun feline
Playfully I take ribbon and start to combine
It with movements to tease the divine
Tugging her hair, nibbling her neckline
Tongue tracing her lacy panty outline
The frothing and groaning are genuine
This is the way I treat a feral feline

# FERRIS WHEEL

He took her into a cage on the Ferris wheel
She knew he would always steal
Her breath away but she loves how she can feel
Free to have a sultry and delicious meal
He started by gently caressing and removing her heel
She was getting very frisky on the Ferris wheel
He wasn't Superman but she saw his steel
Admiration and when he compliments her sex appeal
It does things to her brain when he can't conceal
His desires for her in the air at the top she started to kneel
So much saliva it starts to congeal
He held her upside down like a cartwheel
He played with his doll all over the Ferris wheel

# FLOODING

The way he makes her mind start flooding
With fantasies that make her garden start budding
His large hands easily lifting and hugging
Her into the air and she starts buzzing
Like a bee when he starts sucking
Her lap and he brought a snorkel for the flooding
He knew was imminent because she's becoming
Too turned on with the way he is cupping
Her breasts and his big hands are cutting
Off her air supply, she's loves when he starts roughing
Her up, it always makes her start flooding

# FLOWED

She relaxed, laid back, and as it flowed
In her brain her body felt ready to explode
It got her into the most devilish mode
The deeper he pushed the more it slowed
Down her thinking as her juices flowed
She stuck out her tongue and showed
Him she was ready for her insides to implode
During work she makes naughty videos for him to download
She lived to serve and would do anything to unload
His stress and he busted hotly and immediately started to reload
She was his little filthy commode
Destroying herself in the next episode
He would make her senses totally overload
Now their juices are mixed, the filthy juices flowed

# Freedom

She experiences profound joy in freedom
To express herself openly, it allows her to become
A good girl for daddy, sucking her thumb
Any desire of his she was ready to succumb
To in service, she found new freedom
She's got a lollipop in her mouth, starting to hum
Sparkling hummingbird baby um
You give me feeling when life is plain numb
She's gasping and wiggling as his tongue
Makes her feel ever so young again he's handsome
I make her feel safe and she asks for it in her bum
She loves it covered with saliva for total freedom

# Freezing

She woke up from the cold it was freezing
So, he climbed into her bed and started teasing
Her body his mouth roaming and his hands squeezing
Her body she felt some warmth and it was pleasing
Soon she starts feeling her insides increasing
With fire, he was helping her to stop freezing
The naughtier he becomes, the more liquid starts releasing
She's very worked up now and leaking
Down her leg, how she loves receiving
He whispered I'm close and soon he's leaving
A big deposit on her face and she starts sneezing
Cum, it was so hot how he stopped her freezing

# GAP

She has such a lovely and sexy gap
In between her thighs in her lap
Lurks a filthy monster as she gave one slap
For good luck and another because she would tap
Her face and master uses his bootstrap
The former he becomes, the warmer the gap
His big hands and her throat overlap
He knew where to find her treasure without a map
She's inhaling his mastering while he makes a rap
He tied her up, threw her in the trunk like a kidnap
Into the woods he ties her to a tree as her sap
Is leaking over the forest floor his mousetrap
Sprung quickly grabbing the cheese and missing the trap
She's the queso in his hot chocolate the sweetest gap

# GENTLE

She was floating through the air like a gentle
Butterfly inspired by how he makes her tremble
This man new how to worship her temple
Quickly her panties were in her mouth so temperamental
It gave her darkest desires monumental
Motivation when he starts provoking her mental
Volcano it in fact does not flow out gentle
She explodes everywhere and he's not judgmental
Being able to open fully is incremental
Safety and trust are fundamental
His light touches were almost accidental
He teases her slowly, very gentle

# GENTLY

Today she would not be treated at all gently
Oh, there's a smile on her face she's very friendly
In her mind I unleash the dragon intently
She likes exotic men, those who do it differently
He broke down walls in her mind with rough entry
Then he started licking her mind ever so gently
Making her relax like recess in elementary
School frolicking in the garden planting an assembly
Of perverse thoughts you reap what you sow consequently
She requires difficult punishment from a luxurious gentry
She cries and begs to be used not gently

# GRAVY TRAIN

He showed her how to board the gravy train
He taught her how to adjust to her chain
Her master helper her deeply understand pain
In her head doing things she can't explain
He made her disgusting he made her profane
Invited his friends, all aboard the gravy train
She knew he was crazy, he was far from sane
But he knew just how to lick her brain
That excited her begging to drain
Her master she feels everyone's rain
Covering her, stuffed like a turkey, she's their gravy train

# GUSHING

When she was treated roughly she started gushing
She was ready for anything and nothing
Was too nasty for her, she was something
Of a deviant and started dripping from his loving
Tender caresses and then roughly shoving
It down her throat made her eyes start gushing
Tears of joy and her face is blushing
As all the blood in her body starts rushing
From his harsh blows, his large hands crushing
Her throat deep breaths as she starts huffing
She barks like a dog as he keeps stuffing
Her holes fully which causes lots more gushing

# Hit

Her eyes grew wild as she started to hit
Herself as she slowly scratched her tit
She loves when it gets difficult and it
Kept getting warmer the harder she hit
Herself she was his bitch and ready to admit
That it turned her on to be treated like shit
He ordered her to open her eyes and spit
All over her sheets put the dildo in her ass and started to sit
She's master's bitch and will commit
Herself to do anything and always permit
Her master whatever he wants she will submit
She became a wild unicorn by continuing to hit

# Hot and Heavy

He shaped her definition of hot and heavy
Imagination and suggestions were key
If he starts speaking slowly she
Finds herself gripped with growing glee
He spoke like an angel heavenly
Then he used his body to get hot and heavy
Grabbing his belt putting her over his knee
His hands so firm, his tongue so feathery
She was his very eager and horny pony
Who turned into a unicorn her reality
Becomes better when he makes it hot and heavy

# ICE CREAM

Every day she needed her ice cream
He snuck into her bed as she started to dream
Using his tongue to make her lap steam
She let him do anything, the more extreme
The better so he exploded on her ice cream
Sundae and his hands cut off her airstream
Licking all the cream in her warm seam
Blowing out her back, building her self-esteem
When he smacked her ass, it made her stream
Flowing wildly which he saved to cover her ice cream

# Inner Space

He searched the universe for her inner space
It started with warmth, playing with grace
How he knew just how to make her mind race
She's a perfect ten and he's an ace
At exploring her sparkling inner space
She started melting when he picked up the pace
He encouraged her to wildly debase
Herself and she did everything without disgrace
He sent her to the store with whore written on her face
He was her glowing rose as he sat in her vase
She started biting her lip, she started to brace
For the flurry of invitations at the marketplace
The line keeps growing, there's a race
To be next in line, to be the one to replace
Her lava hot melting leaking all over the place
It's incredibly hot and tight, her inner space

# JILL

There is no other girl quite like Jill
She does things almost nobody else will
Eager to please and determined to fulfill
The wildest fantasies, she begs me to fill
Her full of my cream and uses her mouth to refill
Me and now my balls are full again because of Jill
She loves to submit, loves to thrill
Enjoys most when I start to really drill
Her hotly and always down to chill
Tying her up so she stays very still
My tongue moving slowly uphill
On her mountains of lovely daffodil
I enjoy blowing very lightly on your flower Jill

## LENIENCY

She begged for understanding and leniency
But really, she hates being treated decently
She longed to me made act super indecently
She dreamed if being used roughly repeatedly
The most important thing for her was no leniency
He did things to her that are conceivably
Make her feel too hot, unbelievably
Excited it makes her start behaving obediently
She felt her tits and ass being smacked repeatedly
She begged for it, she said it will go in easily
Gagging her so she gets destroyed peacefully
She no longer cared about her decency
She desired most to get zero leniency

# LESSON

She had just started school, eager for a lesson
Each minute of class causing a new obsession
She opened her legs and asked teacher a question
Sir, what's the best cure for depression
She got instantly wet when he replied, aggression
Now she's in detention for her lesson
When his hand met her face her expression
Was priceless, then he ordered her confession
He folded her body using his body for compression
Then she saw that teacher had brought seven
Other teachers and they used her in quick succession
Being drenched in cum was her new heaven
Teacher whispered tomorrow there will be eleven
Men to give you an even more difficult lesson

## LEVITATE

He held his hummingbird while she started to levitate
He woke her up in the morning when he ate
Her pussy as he ordered her to put the full weight
Of her body on his face, it was his fate
To make it glow at her heavenly gate
He collected her juices on his plate
Of pancakes adding his own cream to satiate
His hungry hummingbird felt great
Sucking his sweetness, she can't wait
To get to the lava center how he can create
The naughtiest thoughts inside her, he makes them levitate

# MESS

She loved when he made her a beautiful mess
Being used roughly relieves her stress
Over his knee she continues to confess
That she gets so hot when he rips her dress
His large hands on her throat start to press
She is becoming undone, she's a hot mess
All her holes were open for him, total access
Slapping her ass roughly, he would caress
Her tits and cause pain to excess
She was eager to do anything to impress
Her master, the dirtiest thoughts posses
Her until she is no longer able to repress
Her filthy urges she couldn't cum unless
He allowed it, in the stadium she will undress
Everyone looking at the wet spot on her dress
Saliva everywhere, they all stare at her mess

# MILKSHAKE

He took her to the mall and bought a lemon milkshake
Then took it in the bathroom dipping his snake
Now she's got a special treat he would make
Her suck his dick each time he would wake
A glass of cum, saliva, and lemon, her milkshake
He brought a friend, and they would take
Turns using her holes doing their best to break
Her ass cream over her face, a filthy cupcake
She leaks everywhere it's impossible to housebreak
This wild pet giving her lap another earthquake
He mixed his cum into the batter, a dirty pancake
She ate so eagerly she got a stomachache
Gagging so hard she threw up her milkshake

# MISCONDUCT

If I'm guilty of anything it would be misconduct
I like things flowing like an aqueduct
She dressed like a student, and I started to instruct
All my favorite ways to corrupt
Little mamacitas make me guilty of misconduct
I love to walk around town with their juices stuck
To my face when ladies smell it so abrupt
She smelt me and said excuse me hate to interrupt
Did you just make something erupt
Indeed, I did watch two mamacitas suck
Each other would you like join in more misconduct?

# Missed

She hadn't read anything spicy lately and missed
The way it made her brain feel kissed
How his words created a light mist
She said you always know how to assist
Me in making me use my wrist
Firm spankings in order to assist
Longings and desires that didn't exist
Until he whispered hot things she couldn't resist
Squeezing her breasts and starting to twist
Her nipples giving pleasure she had always wished
For his tongue to leave not a centimeter missed

# Mist

All over her body was a fine layer of mist
It was totally his fault she was a hedonist
He created temptation impossible to resist
Starting with tying a scarf around her wrist
Soon she will have everything she ever wished
For and just the thought covered her in mist
The firm and harsh slaps came swift
Not a spot on her body was missed
He gave her a naughty surprise twist
Opened her mouth and slowly pissed
In it, she got so hot from his salty mist

# MOLTEN

Her oozing of lava was glowing and molten
His big hands were a thief, her breath was stolen
Yet for some reason other parts of her became quite swollen
She begged him to make her shower golden
The way he treated her seems to embolden
Her to become hot as lava, oozing her molten
Juices he gave her nirvana, she's totally zen
She shuddered and screamed when it happened again
This time it got in her hair and it's dripping down her chin
She's singing his praises, screaming amen
She gets heated thinking of delicious sin
His big hands rubbing her where wise men
Know how to turn holy women into a fountain
Now she's boiling over, her volcano is molten

# MOTHER'S DAY

She is having a fantastic Mother's Day
She has gotten a lovely, fresh bouquet
Of flowers and told her to just lay
Back and be his all you can eat buffet
His tongue expressing his passion with no delay
She got and was breakfast in bed, exceptional foreplay
Exceptional generosity was her favorite gourmet
Dish so she was always eager to obey
He was using his tongue on her engine the raceway
It was shockingly good, her personal stingray
He used her juices to make a souffle
He touches her mind like the sunray
Her hair and body in total disarray
She's having the hottest and naughtiest Mother's Day

## Moving

I spoke to her softly about getting her moving
She listened to how I started slowing
Down her breath and she lays back to soothing
Melodies and my joking is very amusing
I have only one aim to start producing
A chemical reaction that gets her moving
Of all the ideas to start with I am choosing
To do the things that get her body grooving
Her delight and anticipation are improving
Her mood and soon the fire shall be all consuming
My words are sweet because I am using
My tongue to get your mind and body moving

# NEON

He made her put on her smallest neon
Top and a leather skirt and go sit on the lawn
He started ripping her neon nylon
Tights and soon it will be Armageddon
Total destruction highlighted in neon
Her ass and his large firm hands have a swift collision
Rubbing her shamrock and flicking her leprechaun
Hand around her neck making her smile gone
Jumping and cheering, shaking her pompon
Thick, rich, and sticky tastes like Cinnabon
Turned on the blacklight to see my cum glow in neon

# NIGHTS

She was wearing nothing saying nights
In the dark she has very bright headlights
The only thing better than her in tights
Is when she very excitedly jumps and excites
Me as I whisper warm things as she bites
Her luscious lips and imagines several nights
Alone with me reaching new heights
Now she's handcuffed and I'm reading her rights
She loves when he's firm, even more then when he's nice
He starts rubbing her hot body with ice
Which warms her insides in the most precise
Manner that makes it easy to entice
Her open her mind as I fill it with spice
She gets me excited I exploded twice
As much as normal, it's some super-hot nights

# ORGANIC

She was a garden of inspiration, totally organic
They fit together like a puzzle, click
Their bonding blossoming like a botanic
Field of flowers, their connection so dynamic
A sweet little lady admiring his gigantic
Smile and the laughter was organic
She as cool as an iceberg, sinking his Titanic
Wait, she's naturally hot as lava, her volcanic
Beauty inspiring a fusion of thermodynamic
Energy in her mind being a mechanic
It felt so good together, no need to panic
Art inspired by her was extraordinarily romantic
Their admiration of each other beautiful and organic

# PATH

Things kept dropping in her lap, on her path
She smiled, he really made her laugh
He suggested she draw a bubble bath
While he drew her excitement on a bar graph
Which of us will be boss, which will be the staff
The road to their desires making a swerving path
Her thoughts start racing, as his hands massaged her calf
Her pleasure started filling like a carafe
It was adding up quickly, very basic math
Now his rooster is drenched in her birdbath
Water all over the bathroom, the aftermath
Looked like they had been on a warpath
He added more laughter and moisture to her path

# PITBULL

She was his pet, his little Pitbull
He bought the chain and begged him to pull
She begged for all his cum, a whole basketful
She said make me you cum bucket, a whole bucketful
She was thirsty for cum, his hungry Pitbull
He had her treats, a whole pocketful
Nothing excited her like an overwhelming mouthful
She tied her hair in pigtails for master to pull
She wanted all of her holes completely full
All 5 fingers in her mouth, a solid mouthful
He fed her his cum by the spoonful
That's what she desired most, his starving Pitbull

# PLAIN

She is naturally beautiful totally plain
Then I start massaging her brain
All the stress begins to drain
From her body and I am able to obtain
Total clearance she asked me to explain
Again how stunning she is plain
I start talking about fire and she wants propane
Now that she's relaxed, I elaborate on the most profane
Things and it starts driving her totally insane
She groans when my hands are removed as I restrain
My urges to destruction and I know how to entertain
Her curiosity, she had the right to remain
Silent and I will use my imagination plane
Lifting off she's exploding the effects are plain

# PLAYTHING

It is Saturday night and she is his  plaything
She's so light and easy to fling
Around the room he had ordered her to bring
Herself closer as she's massaging his angel wing
This must be heaven sinning so much with my plaything
Grab the back of her head and tell her to sing
Lifting her over my head making her body swing
I slammed her so hard it broke the boxspring
I brought my mask and fins to go snorkeling
It's a wild ocean of fun with my hot little plaything

# PRESSURE

He was under an immense amount of pressure
She got on her knees and started to pleasure
Him using more saliva than ever
She was his filthy pet, his dirty treasure
Now she's breathing through her nose as the pressure
Builds her eyes watering as together
She was taught another dirty lesson from her professor
She screamed all my holes are yours, wherever
You want it I will take you and measure
The tears as he started using his leather
Belt around her neck, extreme pressure

# PRIDE

The Manizalen Mamacitas walk down the street with pride
I asked one if she ever wished that someone spied
On her long enough to openly confide
That she had the world's greatest backside
Her friends giggling as she blushed with pride
That's very original, nobody ever tried
That before and now the mamacitas cried
Out ay ay ay there giggling and cackling multiplied
I picked her up easily like she was my bride
She was giggling and smiled very wide
It made the group of mamacitas decide
To bring me along, a lion with his pride

# Provoker

She was a natural born provoker
Proactive beyond measure I'm her Joker
She's my Harley Quinn and she's wearing a choker
I'm stroking her fire with my poker
Greasing her gears, revving her motor
The best part of firing up a provoker
Is when you light her chimney, it becomes a smoker
The sex so thick the neighbors smell the odor
But it's silent because she begged me to choke her
Balls deep is just about the best way to silence a provoker

# Public

He encourages her to be naughty in public
She soon was his favorite naughty chick
Five fingers in her mouth was his favorite trick
Gagging so hard it almost makes her sick
She is now ready to take on his thick
Member as she swallows him in public
She starts using her mouth to make it slick
Any opportunity to please master she is quick
To do whatever it takes to make his prick
Grow again, she smeared her hot lipstick
All over her naughty professor, her favorite lunatic
He bent her over and she begged him to stick
It in her ass and then back in her mouth in public

# PUNCHING BAG

She felt inspired to be his punching bag
Her tongue sticking out, her ass starting to wag
She said use me to relieve your stress and brag
To all your friends about your slutty punching bag
Her sharp nails across her chest started to drag
Then she started thumping herself like a beanbag
She took her fingers deep as she started to gag
Her master put on his pet's dog tag
He used her clothes as his cumrag
His fingers in her ass as they start to shag
He was penetrating and destroying his punching bag

# RELAXING

He was sitting in his bed, just relaxing
He was woken up with her mouth while napping
She had decided to use his body for snacking
His eyes opened to her firmly slapping
Her face she does it without asking
Now she's using her mouth to keep relaxing
Her master his big hands start grabbing
Her neck as her pussy warms and she is backing
Her ass into his face and he's happily lapping
It she grabs his belt and begs for firm attacking
It gets her so excited when he starts whacking
His little pet puts her ass in the air wagging
Her naughty tongue as she keeps smacking
Herself asking for her treat as he starts jacking
Off into her mouth as he keeps paddling
His filthy dog, her pain helps him in relaxing

# Roughed

He wrote beautiful poetry and he warmly roughed
Up her brain with naughty ideas as he stuffed
Her imagination with ideas that puffed
Up her hottest bits when she felt herself handcuffed
It got her on the edge of her seat he roughed
Up his little doll taking her panties, he stuffed
Her mouth and his large hands crushed
Her throat as she knew that she must
Do the dirtiest things, his belt brushed
Against her backside and all the feelings rushed
To her lap as it started to combust
He did it with passion and appetite very robust
Destruction making wet explosions from being roughed

# Rule

She chose to deliberately disobey the rule
She desired her teacher badly, in school
She would dream of his large body being cruel
To her and making her collect her drool
Her lap needs a towel because it's become a pool
She couldn't resist breaking the rule
He knew how to make her unable to cool
Her jets and she bent over revealing her jewel
Please teacher, please use my favorite tool
Grab the ruler and give me all your fuel
She begged him to empty his very full
Balls and she always swallows, that's the rule

# SALIVATE

It takes good training to make her salivate
The warm rainbow energy her favorite trait
That and knowing how to make her feel great
A patient person that knows how to wait
Until her eyes look like the cat that ate
The canary a little kitten starting to salivate
For thick, rich cream it was fate
That our paths crossed, we are able to create
An easy button to be able to locate
The most sensitive spots on which to fixate
On and use my tongue in a figure eight
Perks her up like Kona coffee come visit 808
Come to Maui with me makes her satiate
All her fantasies together makes her salivate

# SANDWICH

She was smashed between them like a sandwich
Beating her like meat made her such a bitch
Being a nasty whore felt so very rich
They used her holes, then they would switch
Covering her in their sauce, their dirty sandwich
It made her feel alive; they helped enrich
Her life as they took her in a ditch
In the park, she was a wild witch
She explodes everywhere, her body starts to twitch
Grabbing her hair, scratching her nasty itch
To once again be their slutty sandwich

# SEA

She bought her ticket,  she's going to the sea
On an adventure for football which fills her full of glee
She said how many fingers and I said three
Stuffing her ass and licking her fingers repeatedly
She loves when she gets to act obediently
Her sheets would soon look like the sea
She screamed at the stadium, she
Really loves football, as much as being his pony
Her desires to be brutal and smutty
Where boiling over his eager little puppy
Covered in saliva and milk, her new reality
Was she swallows like a mermaid undersea
I order her mouth open and start to pee  ·
It's wet and salty just like the sea

# SIDE

She opened her legs, showing the naughty side
Of her and I whispered let me guide
You, let me make it easy for you to decide
To start opening your mind and legs wide
She pulled her blue panties to the side
Now the churning in my balls is multiplied
She said here's some inspiration, she spied
My growing excitement and begged to ride
Me, she yells anything for you, you won't be denied
So I told her next time to do it outside
I took her in the park and carefully tied
Her to the bench and stuck my tongue inside
Her ass, she loves my devilish side

# Silent

He slipped into her bed totally silent
She had asked to be taken in a violent
Manner so when she found a blue-eyed giant
She begged him to be a disturbing tyrant
She loved obeying, she was totally compliant
Her panties in her mouth while she stays silent
Doing things like this makes her excitement
Go to new levels, her teacher gave her an assignment
He told her to think about enjoying defilement
That she's becoming the baddest girl with refinement
She was his pleasure prisoner and her confinement
Was rich and golden, she's a butt pirate
As his tongue entered her ass she stayed silent

# Sky Moon

She glows in the night that's why she's Sky Moon
Washing her car naked in the afternoon
I'm thirstier than the people in Dune
For just a little drop, just a teaspoon
Of the essence of Miss Sky Moon
She's hotter than Texas in June
That huge smile makes me swoon
She's a butterfly that burst out of her cocoon
Whale done miss, you activated my harpoon
I'd like to wash you until you give me your monsoon
Feral as heck, a car washing racoon
We should open a car wash saloon
Line out the door waiting to see Sky Moon

# SLANT

She had such amazing everything it made my world slant
She wears Minnie Mouse ears and I'm her elephant
She loves playing office, my personal assistant
She watered her desk and started to plant
Herself down on my lunch, my eggplant
She said it will fit inside if you just slant
It downwards my dirty mamacita confidant
Would speak her mind right but right now she can't
She rubbed her magic lamp and started to pant
She knew her naughty genie would only grant
Her one wish so she wished me to enchant
Her and use her body until she walked with a slant

# Sleeping

She snuck into his bed while he was sleeping
He felt her warm little body as the bed started creaking
Being his little doll made her start pleading
Anything aggressive from her master gets her leaking
She filled her mouth fully, no need for speaking
She loved taking advantage of master while he's sleeping
She hovered above his head as she started leaking
Using her juices to slowly start feeding
His perversions and she can see she's succeeding
In waking up parts of him, she loves his excreting
Every day even naughtier, she is succeeding
In being a dog and she loves when he's squeaking
Draining master's balls while he's sleeping

# SLINGSHOT

He was a smooth stone inside a slingshot
He knew just how to make her plot
For her destruction, she dreams of that a lot
It's just the perfect thing to get her filthy hot
His belt around her neck his slingshot
Made her almost pass out as she fought
Her urges, he makes her want to get caught
His loveliest student loves when she's taught
A lesson in discipline and he put a nasty thought
Of her being his whore, he hit her like buckshot
Stroking her clit, getting her jackpot
Then his tongue igniting her yummy hotspot
He filled her completely, emptying his slingshot

# SQUIRT

She needed a towel to catch her squirt
Bouncing on top of him, lifting her skirt
She smiles for the camera, what a flirt
She felt so much pleasure she started to spurt
Now the towel is totally drenched in squirt
She opened her mouth, sir please insert
It in my mouth, destroy your filthy pervert
Make it more difficult, please make it hurt
I like it really rough, treat me like dirt
He starts slapping her tits, lifting her shirt
She felt him filling her up with his yogurt
When he stuck it in her ass, she got very alert
He wanted her hot cream, give me my dessert
Sitting on his face, drenching him with her squirt

# Strategy

There's a very useful and delicious strategy
To melt minds and laps exclaiming thankfully
Making and opportunity out of a tragedy
You're tragically sinful your majesty
A tongue bath until she has great agony
Just where she loves it most, the strategy
Of getting her to act and speak blasphemy
Is to show how wild and rascally
You can be which I am doing now happily
She opens her mind and finds a new galaxy
I am open to just about anything fantasy
If you confess it, we will find a superior strategy

# STRIKING

She has a very pretty face, quite striking
Legs that look like she does a lot of biking
Together on magical mountains we start hiking
It is nice being so open and not hiding
Anything she loves hearing how striking
She is and it makes her start biting
Her lip when he starts creatively writing
Things that touch her heart and keep delighting
Her senses as she admired his deciding
To be totally vulnerable and continue describing
The many ways in which he finds her so striking

# SUCKER

She showed up to detention and pulled out a sucker
She knew how to get her teacher's mind in the gutter
She started shifting in her chair revealing her upper
Thigh as she started to slowly pucker
Her lips and drooling all over her sucker
Now her insides are churning and making butter
In between her legs creamy and wanting teacher to smother
Her she wanted to tempt him, to uncover
His darkest desires, she wanted to discover
How much her teacher would make her suffer
Thinking of him made her lap create a gusher
Now she's dipping it in her lap, a creamy, wet sucker

# Sunflower

On dark days she was a bright sunflower
I spoke highly of her to empower
Her ninja skills she's got great firepower
In her tone legs and is in control of her power
When she smiles it creates warmth like a sunflower
Playing Jimi Hendrix's All Along The Watchtower
As she says I bet that I could overpower
You and I think of her passionflower
Smell and she taunts me that she'll use her superpower
She makes me see more shooting stars than a meteor shower
Today I get to wrestle with a feisty sunflower

## Syrup

He collects her juices to use as his syrup
He watched as she quickly filled a large cup
With his warm words and tongue making her erupt
He dressed a doctor, time for her checkup
He checked her temperature and saw her syrup
Leaking down her leg as he started to pickup
The pace as she longed for this warm-up
He opened her flower, teasing her buttercup
She wanted him to slowly corrupt
Her inhibitions and the juicy buildup
Made her grab her phone and get a close-up
Of the wonderful mess she made as he makes her cleanup
Her juices from the floor, tasting her filthy syrup

# TELLING

Something happens to her when he starts telling
Her how good she looks, and she keeps excelling
In the gym she makes many men start swelling
Which makes her feel swell, he keeps compelling
Her thoughts to get hotter as his hands are dwelling
Over her mouth to quiet her excited yelling
She likes being told what to do he keeps telling
Her things that naughtily start propelling
Her to release her essence she is expelling
Her juices and the whole gym help smelling
Her excitement, her desires are very telling

# THUNDER

It rains a lot in Manizales, but he brought thunder
To her life the way that he woke her from her slumber
Licking her ass and shoving a cucumber
Inside her filled her body and mind with wonder
She hit herself harder and it sounded like thunder
She loves when he grabs her hair and starts to smother
Her thinking of him sliding his hand under
Her panties and start to dial the hottest number
First, she drenches everywhere then he brings more thunder

# Tired

She thought of how very tired
She was and how they admired
Each other so when they retired
They bask in the newly inspired
Dreams they both felt desired
Recharging each other when tired

# TRACK

She looked at him and it got her off track
She thought of last night and had a wild flashback
He was finding her needle in the haystack
St the same time slowly sharing a wisecrack
He was hurdling her bars on the track
Each time his large hands started to smack
Her ass it felt like the world's hardest whack
She smiled and said I want another paperback
Give it to me and take me bareback
Use me until you blow out my holes and back
She cried out in pleasure from his swift attack
Drippings all down the hallway leaving a track

# TURN

She waited patiently for her turn
Watching her friends get disciplined made her yearn
To be able to show master that she could earn
His trust and that she was willing to learn
She wanted harsh treatment, the most stern
Punishment and it was finally her turn
He was the boss, and she dressed as his intern
She longed for her boss so much it gave her heartburn
He gave her lashings and the burn
Stayed on her body for days like a sunburn
She is eager for the next terrifying turn

# TWISTED

She is excited by his depravity, he's so twisted
A true expert in perversions, he so gifted
In the park in the bench his hands drifted
Under her skirt and swiftly he lifted
Her spirits by doing something new and twisted
She enjoyed his ideas so much that she insisted
That she smack her face, she assisted
In her defilement and she has enlisted
Another girl friend to discover things that never existed
Before and they are both tied up and they resisted
Lightly now they were a hot mess consisted
Of lots of saliva mixed with desires most twisted

# Ufff

He knew just how to make her yell ufff
Filling her head with filth, she can't get enough
He encouraged her to do the filthiest stuff
Anything for master, especially if done rough
She starts salivating at the sound of the handcuff
Locking it is making her too wet, ufff
He made it very difficult, her nipples start to puff
She started moaning and barking like a dog, ruff
She wants it to very hard, the more tough
He gets with her the more it makes her go ufff

## Weekend

I wonder what she is doing this weekend
I wonder if she would allow herself to depend
On me making her stretch and bend
Her with sweetness and depravity, the perfect blend
Of temptation she knows I would spend
Days in her lap, I'd lick her all weekend
Making her believe in heaven as we ascend
Time and space as I continue to expend
My energy into her garden as I tend
To frolic in her flower like a bee she tells a friend
About his dedication, my tongue a true godsend
She begged to record it and I dared her to send
It to all her friends now there's a party to attend
It's all her girlfriends versus my tongue this weekend

# WET

She was reading things that got her wet
He knew just how to start to let
Her juices start flying like a jet
On her knees begging him to let her get
Her treat, lots of saliva making it super wet
Pulling her hair, making her sweat
She gets wild dreaming of being his pet
Doing the filthiest things, she'll never forget
He put her into a super slutty mindset
Tears flowing freely but she's not upset
He made her a cum covered omelet
Eating his sauce for breakfast gets her too wet

# WORKING

She was constantly busy, always working
She craves for him to start lurking
In her mind in the gym hotly twerking
Making everyone's jaw drop and smirking
She does enjoy when a man's hardworking
He installed depravity in her mind and it's working
Too well she can't help but squirming
He's so sweet but she begs for more hurting
He made it so difficult for her to stop squirting
His tongue in her lap so hotly flirting
He made her imagine the most disturbing
Things and it gets her too hot, it's really working

# YEARN

I teach her a lot about waiting,  it makes her yearn
For new ways and experiences to learn
Her favorite is when my lessons are stern
My large firm hands make it burn
Everywhere and the heat makes her yearn
For him to call his friends and give them a turn
We fill her as her stomach continues to churn
Not a single man or woman would she spurn
She wants it always, she has a insatiable yearn

www.ingramcontent.com/pod-product-compliance
Lightning Source LLC
Chambersburg PA
CBHW060754180626
46818CB00002B/562